Dream Catcher

by E. Barrie Kavasch
pictures by Gay W. Holland

Richard C. Owen Publishers, Inc.
Katonah, New York

Many of America's native people believe
that the air is filled with good dreams
and bad dreams.

These dreams try to find us
while we are sleeping.

To keep their children safe from bad dreams,
parents and grandparents often make
dream catchers.

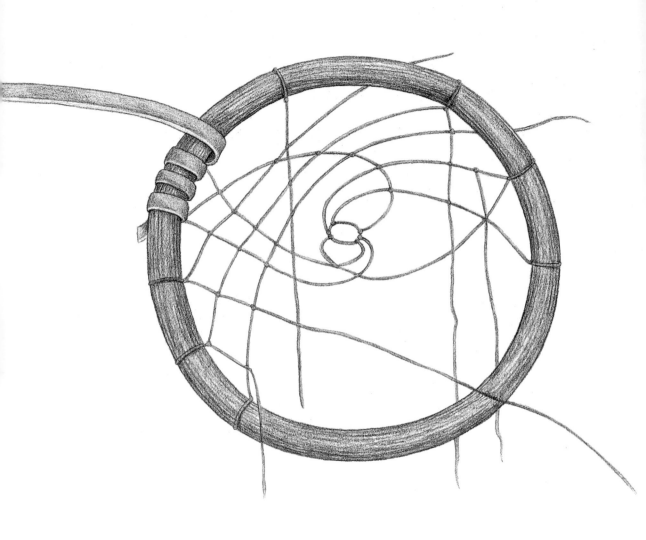

They bend a twig to make a round hoop.
Then they weave strips of leather,
cotton, wool, or silk in a circle
around the hoop and make a web.

Sometimes they add feathers, stones,
or colored beads.

They hang the dream catcher
above the child's bed.

While the child sleeps, the dream catcher
lets good dreams pass through its web
and reach the dreamer.

These are the dreams
of wonderful stories
and beautiful pictures.

Bad dreams, the dreams that frighten children or make them sad, have rough edges.

These dreams get caught in the dream catcher's web.   They are held there and cannot reach the dreamer.

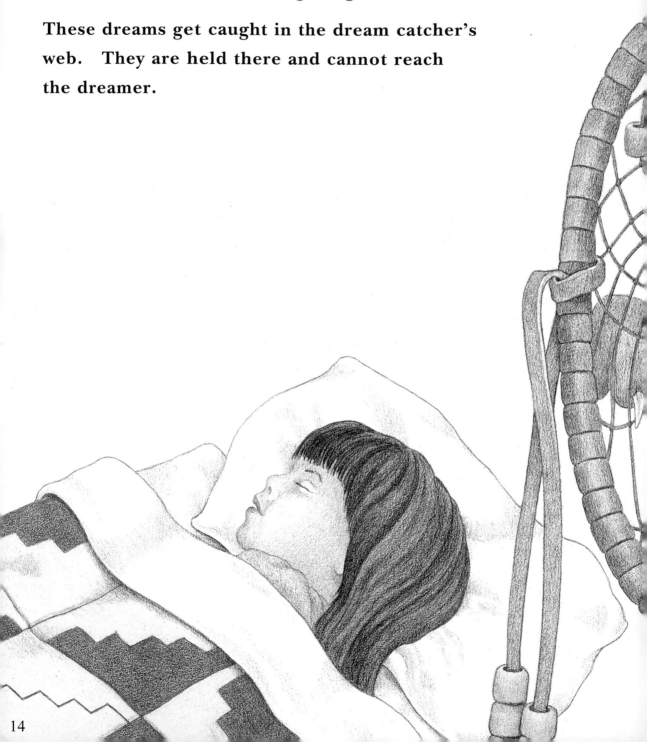

In the morning, daylight comes
and burns the bad dreams away.